STEP 3
STEP · READING ON YOUR OWN

STEP INTO READING®

A STICKER READER

MARC BROWN

ARTHUR IN NEW YORK

WITHDRAWN

Random House 🏠 New York

Visit us on the Web!   StepIntoReading.com   randomhousekids.com

Educators and librarians, for a variety of teaching tools, visit us at RHTeachersLibrarians.com

Library of Congress Cataloging-in-Publication Data
Brown, Marc Tolon.
Arthur in New York / Marc Brown. — 1st ed.
p. cm. — (Step into reading) "A sticker book."
Summary: Arthur and his family, and D.W.'s favorite doll, Mary Moo-Cow, take a vacation to New York City.
ISBN 978-0-375-82976-5 (trade) — ISBN 978-0-375-92976-2 (lib. bdg.)
[1. Brothers and sisters—Fiction. 2. Dolls—Fiction. 3. Vacations—Fiction. 4. Aardvark—Fiction.
5. New York (N.Y.)—Fiction.] I. Title. II. Series.
PZ7.B81618Aldm 2008 [E]—dc22 2007012883

Printed in the United States of America   17 16 15 14 13 12 11 10 9

"Here we are," said Arthur's dad. "The Big Apple Hotel."

"Wow!" said Arthur. "Three days in New York City."

"And Mary Moo-Cow has an outfit for every one," said D.W.

"I love our room," said D.W.

"And all these free snacks."

"They're not free," said Arthur.

"Let's see the city," said Mom.

"And what's city-rule number one?"
asked Dad.

"Don't go off by yourself,"
said Arthur and D.W.

There was so much to see.

"Look!" said Arthur.

"The Empire State Building."

"Look!" said D.W.

"Mary Moo-Cow Palace."

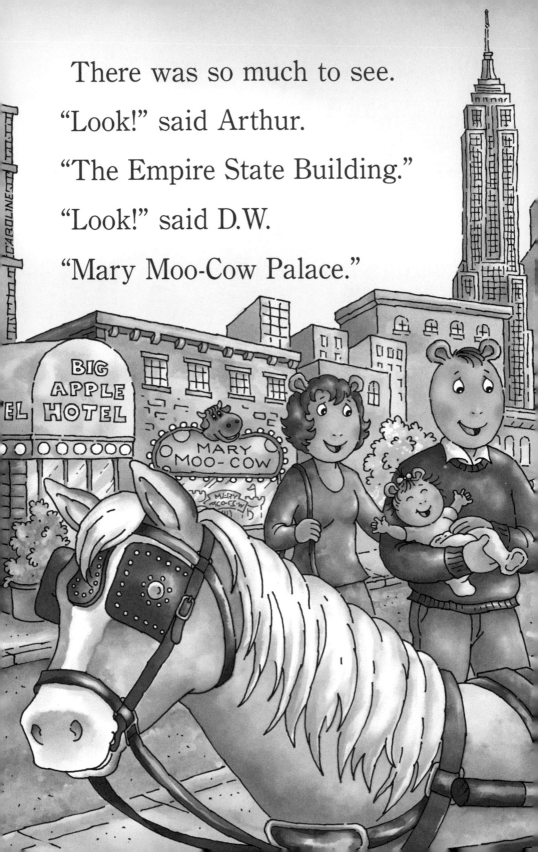

"We'll visit them later," said Mom.
"Who's up for a
    horse-and-buggy ride?"
"Me!" said D.W.
"Let's take the pink one.
    It matches Mary Moo-Cow's
    outfit."

FARES

The next morning,
they visited
the Statue of Liberty.
"Is your doll having fun?"
a policeman asked D.W.

D.W. pressed a button on
Mary Moo-Cow.
"Moooo," said Mary Moo-Cow.
"Oh brother," said Arthur.

In the afternoon, they went
to a museum.

Mom liked the paintings.

10

Dad liked the sculptures.

Arthur liked the mummies.

"Now for something we'll all like,"
said D.W.
"Mary Moo-Cow Palace!"

Mary Moo-Cow Palace had
Mary Moo-Cow everything.

The new Tippy-Toe
Tap Dancer.

The new Star-Bright

Singer outfit.

The Mary Moo-Cow Dream House.

"I could have stayed there for
  hours," said D.W.

"We did," said Arthur. "Let's go."

"But I want to look at Mary's
  window," said D.W.

"Let's come back tomorrow."

"We'll see," said Mom.

But the next day was zoo day.
Mary Moo-Cow wore her
new lion tamer's outfit.

On their last day,
they took a boat trip.
D.W. and Mary Moo-Cow wore
matching outfits.

That evening, they saw
The Lion King.
Arthur liked the songs.
D.W. liked the dancing.

At the end, everyone clapped.

Everyone but Mary Moo-Cow.

She mooed.

"Oh brother," said Arthur.

The three days went so fast!
Now it was time to go home.
"I'll pay the bill," said Mom.
"I'll get the car," said Dad.

"I'll watch Baby Kate,"
said Arthur.
And D.W.?
She had one last thing to do.

"The car is here," said Dad.

"Where's D.W.?" asked Mom.

Mom looked in the gift shop.

Dad looked in the elevator.

D.W. was nowhere to be found.

"I think I know where she is,"
said Arthur. "Follow me!"
They ran out of the hotel
and down the street.

"So there you are, young lady,"
said Mom.

"And what is city-rule number one?"
asked Dad.

"I'm sorry," said D.W. "I just had to
see it one more time."

"You're in big trouble,"
said Arthur.

"I guess Mary and I
will be spending a lot of time
in our room."

"Too bad you don't have
matching prison outfits,"
said Arthur.